WILLIE'S ADVENTURES

Three Stories by MARGARET WISE BROWN
Illustrated by CROCKETT JOHNSON

Willie wanted an animal for his very own. What kind did he want? A little animal. Would he like one that squeaked, asked his grandmother. Yes, that was the very thing. Willie watched for it to come. A big truck stopped. Could it be an elephant? It was a little box. The squeak came out of a hole in the top. What was it?

Willie had a new suit with seven pockets. What should he put in them? His hands? He needed to use his hands. Marbles? He didn't have any marbles. He thought of all the things other people carried in their pockets. Finally he found many nice things to fill his pockets.

Willie walked to see Grandmother. How will I know how to get there, asked Willie. Follow your nose, said his grandmother. Willie did, and had many adventures.

*

WILLIE'S ADVENTURES

THREE STORIES BY
Margaret Wise Brown

Illustrated by Crockett Johnson

THIS SPECIAL EDITION IS PUBLISHED BY ARRANGEMENT WITH
THE PUBLISHERS OF THE REGULAR EDITION
WILLIAM R. SCOTT, INC.
BY
E. M. HALE AND COMPANY
EAU CLAIRE, WISCONSIN

THREE STORIES

Willie's Animal

Willie's Animal

Willie didn't have an animal.
And Willie wanted an animal
to play with.

A real live animal for his very
own.

Because sometimes Willie was lonesome.

There were lots of animals in the country.

So Willie went to the telephone and called up his Grandmother who lived in the country.

"I would like a little animal
for my very own," said Willie.

"What kind of an animal?" asked
his Grandmama.

"A little animal," said Willie.

"A little bird?" asked Grandmama.

"Could you catch one?" asked
Willie.

"I don't think so," said his Grandmama.

"A little horse?" said Willie. "Could you catch me a very little horse, Grandmama?"

"I don't think so," said his Grandmama.

"Are there any wild dogs in the country that would like to belong to someone?" asked Willie.

"They all belong to somebody," said Grandmama.

"And I think you would like a *little* animal to keep in the house," said Grandmama.

"Yes," said Willie. "That's the kind of animal I want—a little animal."

"Would you like one that squeaks?" asked his Grandmama.

"Yes, I would," said Willie.

"Then tomorrow I will send you one," said his Grandmama.

"How will it come?" asked Willie.

"If you wait at the window around noon tomorrow," said his Grandmama, "you will see it arrive."

Then she hung up.

The next morning it was raining.
Big wet drops of water splashed
on the window.

Puddles of water were deep in the
street.

"This would be a nice day to have
a duck," thought Willie.

But out in the country Grandmama
had already put a little animal into
a wooden box and closed the top.
And all you could hear from the
inside was a funny little piping
noise.

"Maybe she will send me a fish,"
said Willie looking out the window
at the big wet puddles.

"This would be a nice day to have a little fish for my very own."

"Or maybe she will send me a little frog," thought Willie.

"I could keep my frog in the puddles."

The big wet raindrops splashed and broke on the windowpane.

"But I think I would like a little animal that I could keep in the house with me," thought Willie.

"Perhaps Grandmama will send me a ladybug."

"A ladybug would be a good thing to have in the house."

"Or perhaps she will send me a little squirrel that I could keep in the piano."

Then, suddenly at noon, the sun came out.

And up to Willie's house came a big truck. It was enormous.

"Oh, my Heavens!" thought Willie, "Grandmama must have sent me an elephant."

The truckman jumped out of the truck, ran around, and flung open the back doors.

The truck was full of horses.
But he didn't take out a horse.
Nor did he take out an elephant.
He took out a little tiny wooden
box.

And he brought the box in to
Willie.

"Open it up, Willie," said the
truckman.

"It has your name on it. Your

Grandmama asked me to bring it
to you."

Then he put down the box and
walked out again, as quickly as he
had walked in. He jumped in his
truck and roared away.

But nobody was at home that noon.
And Willie didn't know how to

open that strong wooden box, which was all nailed down.

And he couldn't see into the box because the cracks were too little and it was too dark in there.

But Willie could hear something moving in the box.

And he heard a high, piping little squeak.

What could it be? Maybe it was a goose.

Maybe it was a lamb.

Maybe it was a rabbit.

The thing seemed to scratch and rattle around a lot in the box.

"Maybe it's a porcupine," said
Willie, as he shivered.
"At any rate," said Willie,
"whatever it is, it's my own."

And he sat down beside the
box and waited, and listened.
He was waiting for his
mother to come home for lunch.
At last she came.

And she got a hammer, and she got a screwdriver.

And they pried open the box.

And out jumped a wild little ball of fur, with long whiskers and bright

green eyes, and sharp white teeth
and a bushy tail.

It was Willie's animal.

"Catch it," said his mother, "it's
your animal."

And Willie went over and caught
the little fur kitten in his arms.

And the kitten began to purr, and
Willie held it very close and very
quiet, with his hand underneath it
so that it wouldn't be afraid of
falling.

And Willie's animal was as happy
as Willie.

Now Willie had his animal.

"If it's my animal," said Willie, "I'll have to take care of it."

"And I would like to give it something to eat."

So Willie and his mother gave the kitten a little dish of milk.

"Now," said his mother, "you might give it a little garden to run around in."

So Willie and his mother fenced in a little garden for the kitten for her very own.

"And now," said Willie, "where will it sleep?"

"You might make it a little bed,"
said his mother.

So Willie took a pillow and put
the pillow in a box.

He put the kitten on the pillow.

And then he took the box up to his own room.

And the kitten went to sleep in Willie's room in the kitten's bed.

And Willie went to sleep in his own bed.

And Willie and his animal took a long nap.

And after they had slept a lot, they ran around in the garden.

And they both grew and Willie named his animal "Grandcat" after his Grandmother.

Willie's Pockets

Willie's Pockets

One day Willie got a new suit.
It had seven pockets.
Three pockets in the coat and
four in the pants.

"What are these all for?" asked
Willie.

"To put things in," said his
father.

"But what shall I put in them?"
asked Willie.

"You'll find plenty of things to

put in your pockets," said his
father.

And off went Willie's father to
work and left Willie with a whole
day ahead of him.

And seven empty pockets.

What to put in them?

Willie walked around the room.

He put a lump of sugar in one
pocket.

But then he got hungry and ate
the sugar.

And his pockets were empty again.

Then Willie walked out of his
house.

Outside was his little kitten.

He tried to put the kitten in his pocket, but his little kitten wouldn't stay there.

So Willie's pockets were empty again.

Seven pockets and all of them empty.

Bzzzzzzzzzzzzzzzzzzzzzzz!

Willie caught the mosquito and
put it in his pocket.

But the mosquito bit him, and so
Willie threw it out.

And his pockets were empty again.

Willie walked down the road to
the edge of the river.

There he met an old man who was fishing.

"What have you got in *your* pockets?" asked Willie.

"Fish hooks and grasshoppers," said the old man. "What have you got in your pockets?"

"Nothing," said Willie.

"What's the matter with you?"
asked the old man. "Seven pockets
and all of them empty?"

"I don't know what to put in my
pockets," said Willie.

"Put your hands in your pockets,"
said the old man.

Willie did.

But pretty soon Willie needed his hands.

So he took them out.

And his pockets were empty again.

"Pockets," said Willie. "What good are seven empty pockets?"

And he sat down on a log and he thought of all the pockets in the world.

"What do other people put in their pockets?"

He thought of men's pockets with money in them and handkerchiefs.

And of big kangaroos with little kangaroos in their pockets.

And of big boys with marbles and
knives in their pockets.

And of his mother's pockets with

safety pins and pieces of paper,
keys, and handkerchiefs.

And of soldiers' pockets with
bullets in them and handkerchiefs.

And of postmen's pockets, and of
sailors pockets.

And of policemen's pockets with
whistles in them.

He thought of all the pockets in
the world.

And they all had something in
them.

"They all have handkerchiefs in
their pockets," said Willie.

And so he went home and got a

handkerchief and put it in his top
front pocket.

"And people have things that they
like in their pockets," said Willie.

He went down to the beach and
picked up some little yellow shells,
and a useful cork, and some round
shiny pebbles, and a piece of green
bottle glass.

He put all these in his two back
pockets.

"And people have things that they

need in their pockets," said Willie.

So he found a piece of string
and put it in his side pocket.

"And sometimes people have
things to eat in their pockets,"
he said, watching a little squirrel
climb a tree.

Willie reached down and picked
up some nuts.

Then he climbed up a tree and
picked an apple.

And he put the nuts and the apple
in his other side pocket.

"And something to play with," said Willie.

He looked all around him.

There in the long grass was a little green shiny marble some boy had lost.

So Willie put it in his pocket.

"And pockets are to keep things in," said Willie.

Then he remembered a gold medal that his Grandfather had once given him.

And he went home and he put that in his pocket.

He put the gold medal in a pocket

that had a zipper, so he wouldn't
lose it.

Then, just as the sun went down,
his father came walking home.

"What have you got in all your
new pockets?" he asked.

"They are all full," said Willie.

And he pulled everything out of his pockets and showed his father.

And he gave his father one of the shells to keep.

"What have you got in *your* pockets," asked Willie.

And his father showed him all the things he had in his pockets.

And he gave Willie one of his keys for his very own.

"It unlocks the front door of the house," said Willie's father. "Don't lose it."

Then they both put their hands

in their pockets and went for a
walk.

And Willie's father taught him
to whistle like a bird.

Willie's Walk

Willie's Walk

Willie lived in a small town.
His Grandmama lived in the country.
She telephoned him.

"Come to see me," said Grandmama.

"When?" asked Willie.

"Now," said Grandmama.

"How will I get there?" asked
Willie.

"Walk," said Grandmama.

"Through the country?" asked Willie.

"Through the country," said Grandmama.

"All by myself?" asked Willie.

"All by yourself," said Grandmama.

"I've heard that wild flowers are wild," said Willie.

"They are," said Grandmama, "but come anyway."

"How will I find the way?" asked Willie.

"Follow your nose," said his Grandmama.

"How will I know when I get to your house?" asked Willie.

"Look inside and you will see me there," said Grandmama.

And she hung up.

So Willie put on his new suit and
he started out.

He walked out of the town and
into the country.

He followed his nose.

The very first thing that he saw
was a *wild flower*.

Should he turn around and go
back home?

No. Not Willie.

He leaned down and sniffed.

It smelled like a violet, so he
picked it.

And Willie walked on to Grandmama.

The country looked very big to Willie.

There were butterflies in the country.

The butterflies fluttered all around his head.

Willie had never seen a butterfly before.

Should he turn around and go back home?

No. Not Willie.

He stood stone still until the butterflies fluttered by.

Then he picked some smelly

weeds that butterflies wouldn't like.

And Willie walked on to Grandmama.

Then he came to three wild red strawberries.

They were almost hidden beneath some very green leaves.

But was Willie afraid of a wild strawberry?

No. Not Willie.

He picked all three strawberries and ate two of them.

The other one he put in his side pocket, so it wouldn't get squashed.

And Willie walked on to Grandmama.

Soon he came to a shallow stream across the road.

There was no bridge.

How would he ever get across?

Should he turn around and go back home?

No. Not Willie.

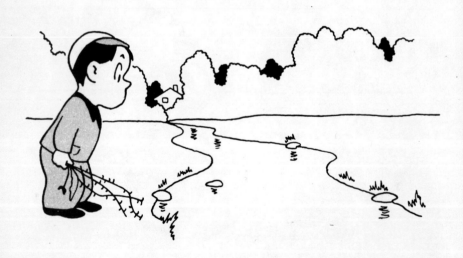

He took off his shoes and socks.

He rolled up his new pants.

And, barefooted, he waded right through the cold, wet water of the stream.

Then he put on his socks and his shoes.

And Willie walked on to Grandmama.

He came to a hill.
It was a very high hill.
Should he turn around?
No. Not Willie.
He walked up the hill backwards,
so as not to see how high it was.

Then he walked down the hill
backwards, so he could see how high
the hill had been.

And Willie whistled as he walked
on to Grandmama.

At last he came to a great big
house. It had enormous doors.
Could this be Grandmama's
house? Willie went and peeked
in the enormous doors.

The house was full of horses.
No Grandmama.

Next he came to a rather small house.

It had a little round door in it.

Could this be Grandmama's house?

Willie went and peeked in the little round door.

The house was full of a big fat dog—sound asleep.

No Grandmama.

Then he came to a tiny little house.

It had a tiny, tiny door.

Could this be Grandmama's house?

Willie went and tried to peek in, but the door was too small.

He heard a quiet buzzing noise
inside, so he knocked to see who
lived there.
Honey bees!
No Grandmama.

Then he came to a white house, all
covered with red roses.

It had a green door and a chimney
with smoke coming out.

Could this be Grandmama's house?

Willie went and peeked in one of the windows.

And there was Grandmama, sitting inside, waiting for Willie to come.

"Sakes!" said Grandmama. "Don't

stand there. Come on in, child."

And Willie went inside and gave
his Grandmama a great big hug.

Then he gave her the wild flower
and the bunch of smelly weeds.

"Very pretty," said Grandmama.
And she gave Willie a glass of

milk and a great big piece of
chocolate cake.

"Oh," said Willie. "Here is a
little wild strawberry for you."

And that was Willie's walk
to Grandmama.